Extreme

Big Beasts

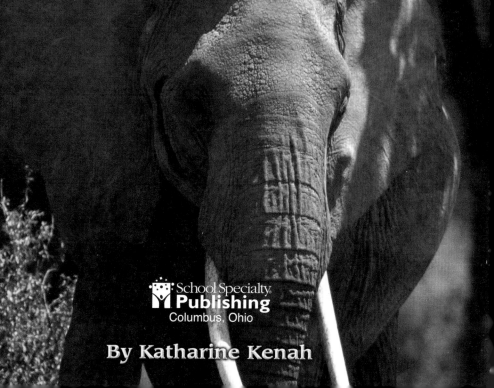

School Specialty
Publishing
Columbus, Ohio

By Katharine Kenah

Copyright © 2007 School Specialty Publishing, a member
of the School Specialty Family.

Library of Congress Cataloging-in-Publication Data is on file with the publisher.

Send all inquiries to:
School Specialty Publishing
8720 Orion Place
Columbus, OH 43240-2111

ISBN 0-7696-4335-3

2 3 4 5 6 7 8 9 10 PHX 10 09 08 07

Animals are all around you.
Some animals are
too small to see.
Some animals are big beasts!

Blue Whale

The blue whale is the biggest
animal in the world.
It is as long as
three school buses.

Giraffe

The giraffe is the tallest
animal in the world.
It is about as tall as
a two-story house.

African Elephant

The African elephant is
the biggest animal on land.
It weighs as much as
two pickup trucks.

Goliath Beetle

The goliath beetle is one of the biggest bugs in the world. It is about as big as your hand.

Giant Squid

The giant squid is the biggest
animal with no backbone.
Its eyes are the size
of dinner plates.

13

Komodo Dragon

The Komodo dragon is
the biggest lizard in the world.
It is longer than
a picnic table.

Crocodile

The crocodile is the biggest reptile in the world.
It is longer than two bikes.

Ostrich

The ostrich is the biggest
bird in the world.
Its eggs are the size
of footballs.

Anaconda

The anaconda is the biggest
snake in the world.
It is about as long
as a garden hose.

Saint Bernard

The Saint Bernard is one of the biggest dogs in the world. It weighs as much as a full-grown man.

23

Siberian Tiger

The Siberian tiger is
the biggest cat in the world.
It is as long as two bathtubs.

Whale Shark

The whale shark is the biggest fish in the sea. Its mouth is as wide as a teacher's desk.

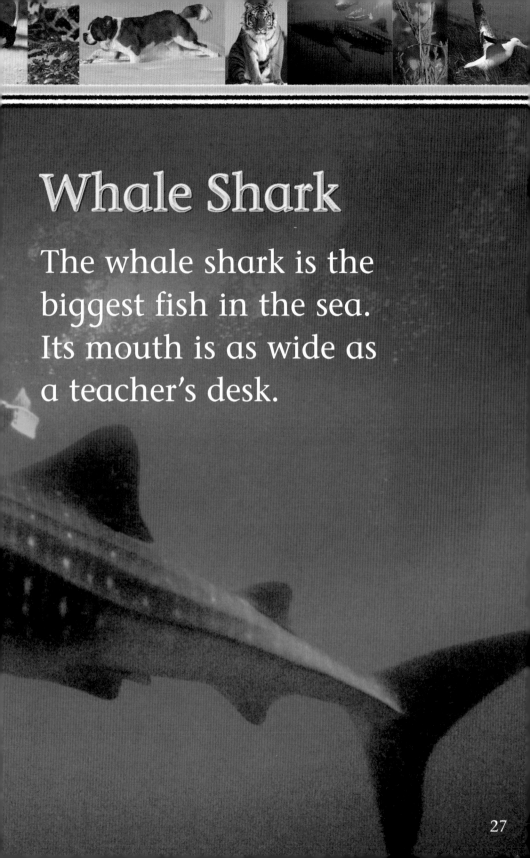

Stick Insect

The stick insect is the longest insect in the world. It is about as long as a ruler.

Albatross

The albatross is one
of the biggest seabirds.
Its spread wings are about
as wide as a two-lane road.

EXTREME FACTS ABOUT BIG BEASTS!

- The blue whale is the largest animal that has ever lived on earth. It is even bigger than the dinosaurs were.

- A giraffe's tongue can grow to be 18 inches long, about as long as your arm.

- An elephant can smell a person more than one mile away.

- A goliath beetle is so big that it sounds like a small helicopter when it flies.

- The longest giant squid on record was 59 feet long, almost as long as a bowling alley lane.

- A Komodo dragon eats 80 percent of its weight in food each day.

- A crocodile's brain is the size of a walnut.

- It would take 24 chicken eggs to equal the weight of one ostrich egg.

- Saint Bernards were once used to rescue people lost in snowstorms.

- A Siberian tiger is big and strong enough to drag prey that would take 12 men to move.

- A whale shark can grow to be 46 feet long, longer than three cars.

- The anaconda is the heaviest snake in the world. It can weigh 500 pounds, as much as a full-grown male lion.

- The longest recorded stick insect was over 12 inches long, about as long as a loaf of bread.

- An albatross can fly for years without returning to land. When an albatross gets tired, it rests on a boat.